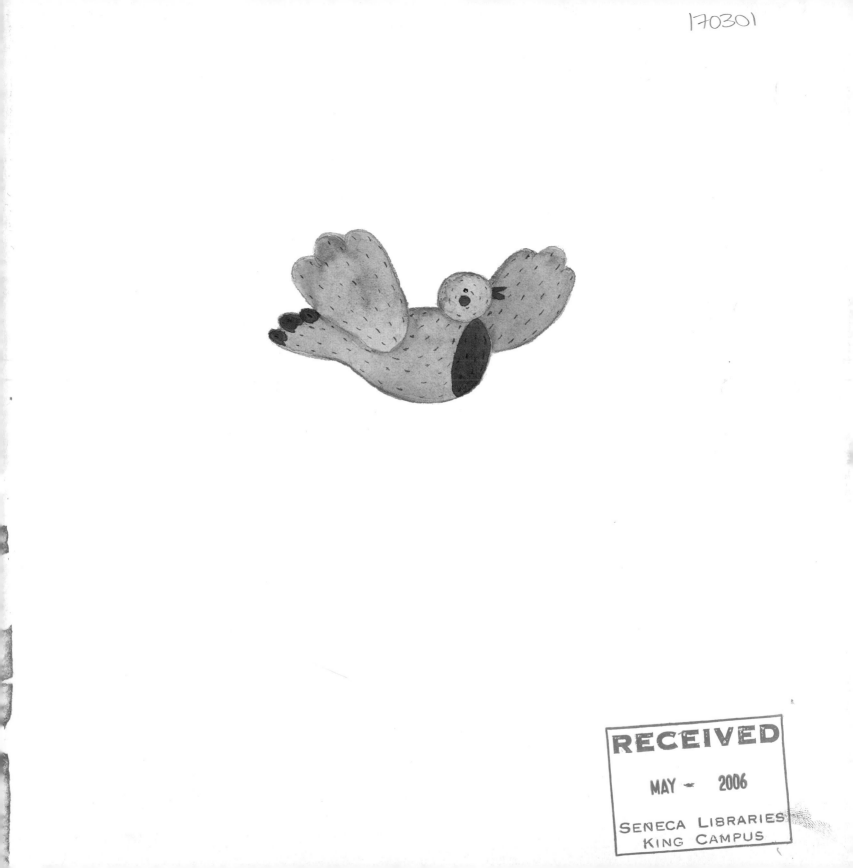

For Hélène

Copyright © 2005 by Mireille Levert
English translation copyright © 2005 by
Groundwood Books

No part of this publication may be reproduced,
stored in a retrieval system or transmitted, in any
form or by any means, without the prior written
consent of the publisher or a licence from The
Canadian Copyright Licensing Agency (Access
Copyright). For an Access Copyright licence, visit
www.accesscopyright.ca or call toll free to
1-800-893-5777.

Groundwood Books / House of Anansi Press
720 Bathurst Street, Suite 500
Toronto, Ontario M5S 2R4
Distributed in the USA by Publishers Group West
1700 Fourth Street, Berkeley, CA 94710

We acknowledge for their financial support of our
publishing program the Canada Council for the
Arts, the Government of Canada through the Book
Publishing Industry Development Program
(BPIDP) and the Ontario Arts Council.

Library and Archives Canada Cataloguing in
Publication

Levert, Mireille
Eddie Longpants / Mireille Levert.

ISBN 0-88899-671-3

I. Title.

PS8573.E956355E32   2005   jC813'.54
C2005-90425-8

The illustrations are in watercolor and
gouache acrylic on Lanaquarelle paper.

Printed and bound in China

Translated from the French by Sarah Quinn

Eddie Longpants

story and pictures by

Mireille Levert

A GROUNDWOOD BOOK / HOUSE OF ANANSI PRESS
TORONTO   BERKELEY

Warning: This book may give you a stiff neck.

*E*ddie Longpants' legs are long.
Really long.
And his feet are enormous.
His gangly arms dangle down
from his shoulders
and bump into everything.
He's big. Really big.

Too big for his locker at school.
Too big for the stairs.
Too big for his desk.
No matter how much he twists and turns,
he's always folded up or bent over,
his nose squished against his shoes.

At recess, no one wants to play with Eddie Longpants.

"Giraffe alert!" shouts Pete.

"Hey, ostrich neck!" hollers Felix.

"No flagpoles allowed!" cries Anna.

"Elephant!" adds Jeremy, who, as usual, just doesn't get it.

So Eddie, with a heavy heart,
sidles up under his favorite tree.
He stands very still.
A little bird approaches,
then another.
They land on his head,
ruffling their feathers
and chirping happily.
And Eddie hums along with them.

The next day, at recess,
the clamor starts again.
"Look, it's the walking staircase!"
cries Pete.
"No, it's Mrs. Ladderhead!" Felix shouts.
"Wait, I think it's a skyscraper!"
shrieks Anna.
Eddie isn't ignoring them.
He's just not listening.

Today is report card day.
Parents file through the classroom.
Everything's fine...
until Eddie's mother arrives.
She's tall. Really tall.
And she's wearing a really big hat!
"We can't possibly meet in the classroom,"
Miss Snowpea says to herself.
So, in a flash, she climbs up to the roof.

Miss Snowpea and Mrs. Longpants talk.
They look each other straight in the eye.
They say nice things.
They smile big smiles.
They shake hands.
Goodbye, Mrs. Longpants.

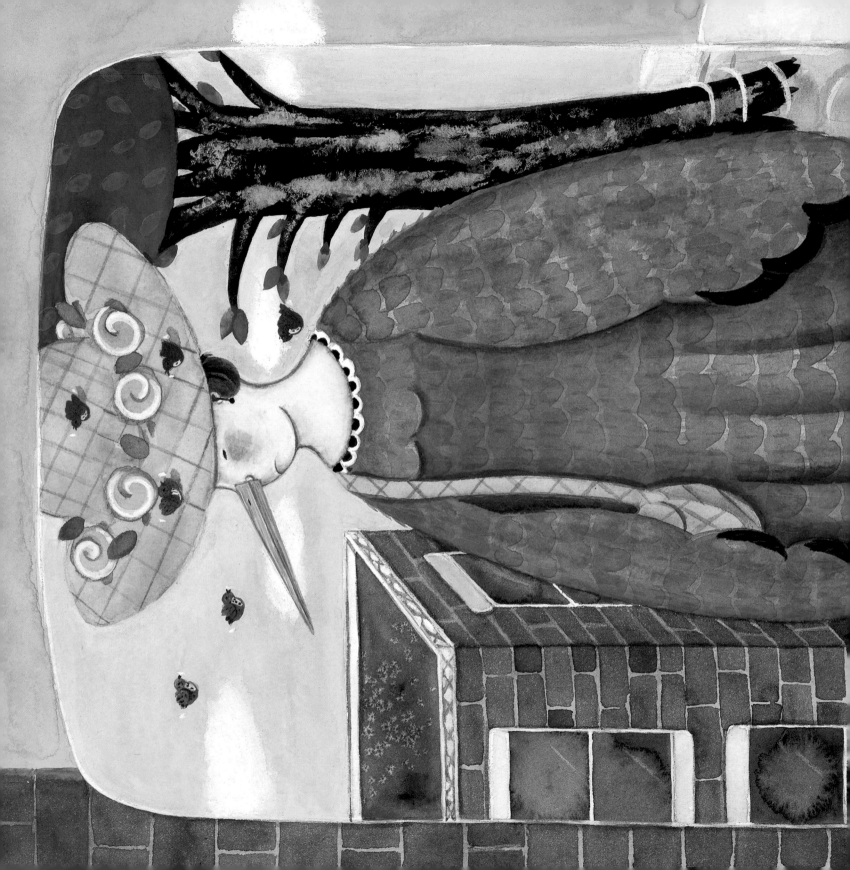

The next day at recess,
Pete lets loose.
"Mrs. Longpants looks like a
heron in a hat!
Mrs. Longpants looks like a big
ugly camel!"
Eddie forgets all about his tree.
He doesn't hear the birds
anymore.
He is in pain.
Enough is enough.

This time, Miss Snowpea hears
Pete's insults.
She feels anger rising inside her.
It makes her insides growl
and her toes curl up.
All this because Eddie is big!

Miss Snowpea is as red as a tomato.
Where is Pete? she wants to know.
But Pete has disappeared into thin air.
He's scared of Miss Snowpea,
especially when she gets angry.

Pete climbs higher and higher
until he's reached the top.
He's trembling all over.
He feels dizzy.
He wants to come down.
"Help! Please, help!" he sobs. "I'm going to fall!"

Eddie makes a phone call, just one,
and help rushes to the scene
in a beautiful red truck.
Mr. Longpants is a fireman!

He sends out the huge ladder
and Eddie climbs up.
He's not afraid.
He reaches out and takes Pete
gently in his arms,
the way only a giant knows how.

A few days later,
the leaves stir gently
in the tree.
The birds twitter.
And Pete, seated firmly on
Eddie's shoulders, says,
"You're a big guy,
that's for sure.
But your heart is even
bigger!"

The End
(of your stiff neck)